# Little Red Riding Hood

**Nick Sharratt**      **Stephen Tucker**

MACMILLAN CHILDREN'S BOOKS

Little Red Riding Hood's mum said,
"Your gran's been on the phone.
She's feeling rather poorly
And she's had a little moan.

"So would you be a sweetheart,
Pop over right away,
And take this shopping with you,
It would really make her day."

Now to get to Granny's cottage
The only way to go
Was through the deep dark forest,
But was she scared? Oh no!

In fact, she wandered off the path
To where the bluebells grew.
Then suddenly a wolf leapt out
And said, "How do you do?"

Red Riding Hood said to the wolf,
"I'm on my way to see
My granny, who is ill in bed."
The wolf cried, "Dearie me!"

He asked, "Where does
   your granny live?"
She pointed, and he smiled.
"It's time that I was on my way,"
He said. "Goodbye, my child."

The wolf had got an evil plan
To eat Red Riding Hood.
And so he raced
    to Granny's house
As quickly as he could.

He jumped in
    through a window,
Snatched the cap
    off Granny's head,
Shoved her in a wardrobe
And leapt into her bed.

When Red Riding Hood came in
She couldn't help but stare.
"Goodness, Gran, you do look strange.
You've grown a lot of hair.

"And your eyes, they look so big,
They've changed from blue to black."
"All the better to see you with,"
The cunning wolf growled back.

Red Riding Hood said, "Poor old Gran,
Your throat must be so sore.
For you to sound as bad as that
You're not yourself for sure.

"And your ears have grown as well,"
She gasped, "I wonder why?"
"All the better to hear you with,"
Came the hoarse reply.

"Come closer, dearest," grinned the wolf,
"And give your gran a kiss."
"You never," squeaked Red Riding Hood,
"Had teeth as big as this!"

"All the better to eat you with!"
Wolf roared with all his might.
He threw aside the duvet
And he tried to take a bite.

Round and round the room they ran,
He pounced and seized her cape.
Poor Red Riding Hood was trapped.
Wolf snarled, "There's no escape!"

He was just about to eat her
When her dad came bursting in.
He'd been chopping logs for firewood
When he heard the frightful din.

First published 2001 by Macmillan Children's Books
This edition published 2021 by Macmillan Children's Books
an imprint of Pan Macmillan
The Smithson, 6 Briset Street, London EC1M 5NR
EU representative: Macmillan Publishers Ireland Limited,
Mallard Lodge, Lansdowne Village, Dublin 4
Associated companies throughout the world
www.panmacmillan.com

ISBN: 978-1-5290-6896-2

1 3 5 7 9 8 6 4 2

A CIP catalogue record for this book is available from the British Library.

Read by Anna Chancellor

Printed in China

MIX
Paper from
responsible sources
FSC
www.fsc.org
FSC® C116313